The Perfect Fall

A Righteous Wrong Origin Story

Walden Gray

waldengray.com

For my family . . .

What I must do is all that concerns me, not what the people think... It is easy in the world to live after the world's opinion; it is easy in solitude to live after our own; but the great man is he who in the midst of the crowd keeps with perfect sweetness the independence of solitude.

Ralph Waldo Emerson

Author's Note

Dear Reader,

Every villain has an origin story. In book one of the *Righteous Wrong* series, *The Emancipation Job*, we met Lolita as an antagonist—cold, calculating, and ruthlessly efficient in her control of others. This prequel aims to explore how she became that person, tracing her journey from ambitious young gymnast to the architect of a system designed to trap and exploit others.

While this story provides context for Lolita's actions, it does not seek to excuse them. Rather, it examines how trauma and the pursuit of control can transform someone, how the abused can become the abuser, and how the quest for perfection can lead us down dark paths.

Through Lolita's story, we see how small compromises and justifications can gradually reshape someone's moral compass. We witness the price of absolute control—not just for those controlled, but for the one wielding that power.

I hope this origin story adds depth to the *Righteous Wrong* series while prompting reflection on how our past shapes us—and how we choose to let it shape others.

Thank you for joining me on this journey into the heart of darkness.

With gratitude,

Walden Gray

Contents

Prologue   1

1. The Young Fighter   3

2. Reinvention   14

3. The Rise   28

4. The Foundation Cracks   42

Afterword   57

Acknowledgements   59

About the author   60

Prologue

L olita watched the wall of monitors before her, each screen a window into someone else's private hell. Twenty-seven cameras, twenty-seven stories, twenty-seven lives under her absolute control. Her perfectly manicured nail tapped against a screen showing a young actress crying in her room, mascara streaking down her cheeks as she clawed at the electronically locked door.

"First night's always the hardest," she said, savoring the girl's desperation like a fine wine. The cameras never blinked, never slept, never missed a single betrayal or moment of weakness. Nearby, two performers whispered, believing themselves unseen. Lolita's lips curled into a predatory smile. Nothing escaped her watchful gaze; all secrets lay exposed. She'd learned long ago that true power lay not in the punishment, but in the anticipation of it.

Her intercom buzzed. "Lolita? There's a situation at the front gate. Parents with a court order. They're threatening to call the police."

Lolita's smile widened as she flexed her sculpted abs, her body still a weapon honed by years of ruthless discipline. Let them rage against her fortress of rules and regulations. She had built this empire on the ruins of her own broken dreams, mortared with the crushed spirits of countless aspiring stars. No one—not desperate parents, not rebellious actresses, not even her own haunting doubts—would tear it down.

Chapter One

The Young Fighter

L olita balanced on the beam, her body a study in precision and control. She moved through her routine with calculated grace, each twist and flip perfectly executed. Her eyes never left the four-inch plane of padded wood beneath her feet. The beam was her world, her sole focus.

She launched into a back handspring, feeling the satisfying impact of her shoulders on the beam and the power coiled in her core. She stuck the landing—naturally—and a smirk tugged at her lips.

At the edge of the mat, Lolita's mother watched, unblinking, a hawk zeroing in on its prey. Natalya Petrov—former Olympic hopeful and current taskmaster extraordinaire; her gaze dissected every angle and line of Lolita's body, searching for the slightest hint of imperfection.

Lolita could feel that stare like a physical weight, but she refused to let it throw off her rhythm. Tall for a gymnast at 6-feet tall, she moved into a switch leap, soaring through the air with legs split at 180 degrees.

The added height accentuated the sharp precision of her technique. The fluorescent lights glinted off her blonde hair, pulled back in its signature tight bun.

***

A memory flashed unbidden: twelve-year-old Lolita, hands raw and bleeding from hours on the uneven bars, fighting back tears as she prepared for another routine. "Again," her mother's voice cracked like a whip across the empty gym. "And this time, don't embarrass me with that sloppy form. You must learn to control your body. Never forget, without control, you're nothing." Lolita's shoulders burned, her fingers screaming in protest, but she chalked up anyway. Weakness wasn't an option . . . it never was with Natalya Petrov watching.

***

"Higher," Natalya barked from the sidelines. Always *higher*, always *better*. Lolita absorbed the criticism silently, using it as fuel. She was a machine, and machines didn't have feelings. They just performed.

She transitioned into her dismount—a double back tuck. Twisting, flipping, defying gravity with apparent ease. Feet slammed into the mat with the finality of a judge's gavel. Stuck it cold.

Lolita held her finishing pose for a moment, arms raised in a *V*, before relaxing into a stance that somehow still looked regimented. She finally allowed herself to meet her mother's eyes, steeling herself for the inevitable onslaught.

But Natalya just gave a curt nod, her face an inscrutable mask. "Adequate," she said, "for now."

High praise, coming from her. Lolita experienced a brief moment of something akin to pride . . . before she quickly suppressed it. Pride was weakness, and weakness was unacceptable. There was still work to be done, routines to drill, muscles to hone into weapons of mass perfection.

This was her life, her purpose, and she would execute it flawlessly—no matter the cost. She had been forged in the crucible of her mother's expectations, tempered by the unyielding demands of the sport. Lolita was many things—ruthless, disciplined, cunning, but above all, she was a survivor. And she would keep surviving, keep excelling, until she stood alone at the top of the podium. Gold around her neck and ice in her veins . . . just the way she liked it.

***

The locker room was a sanctuary of sorts, a dimly lit maze of lockers and weary sighs as girls more than half her age peeled off their disguises, revealing the callused hands and braces underneath. Lolita, however, was already out of her practice gear and into her team warm-ups, having learned long ago that every second mattered.

She laced up her shoes, her movements mechanical and efficient, her mind a whir of calculations. Her mother's critique replayed itself in her head, each word dissected and analyzed for ways to improve. The beam had been good—what word had she used? Oh yeah, *adequate*. Adequate performance from her was great by anyone else's standards, but in this world, *great* meant *mediocre*.

And Lolita was anything but mediocre.

She glanced up at her reflection in the mirror, noting the lack of emotion on her face. Her mother's work, again—an unintended side effect of a lifetime of unrelenting pressure. Lolita was so used to masking her emotions, even when alone, that she couldn't remember the last time she'd allowed herself to feel anything other than cold, calculated determination.

It didn't matter. Weakness was not in her DNA, hadn't been since she'd first set foot on a balance beam at the tender age of five. Gymnastics was a sport that demanded perfection or nothing, and Lolita was far from the *nothing* type.

She slung her gym bag over her shoulder and pushed through the locker room doors, her footsteps eclipsed by the pounding bass of music and the never-ending chatter of girls, all of them vying for the spotlight that seemed just out of reach.

Lolita, on the other hand, knew how to steal the show.

***

The next day on her way home from school, the sun was still high over the Malibu coastline; she asked her driver to stop near the Malibu Pier. She took in the breeze carrying the faint scent of salt and suntan lotion. The suffocating smell reminded her of a life she could have had if she hadn't been born into greatness.

Lolita's parents were both Olympic medalists, their trophies lining the family room like a gauntlet of expectations she'd been running from her entire life. Somehow, even though she could flawlessly execute the Cheng on the vault, it still wasn't enough.

Their compound loomed in the distance, a fortress of white marble and tinted glass, a testament to their success and her failure.

Lolita breathed in the salty air one more time, gathering the last remnants of her resolve before striding towards the sleek, black SUV that awaited her in the driveway.

The driver opened the door for her, and she slid inside, letting the cool leather envelop her like a familiar embrace.

"Home, Lolita?" the driver asked, his voice devoid of any inflection.

She hesitated, her hand hovering over the door handle. Home. The word left a bitter taste in her mouth, like stale success and rusted dreams.

"No," she said, her voice steely with determination. "Time to lift. Take me to the gym."

And with that, Lolita left her past behind, once again chasing the elusive high of perfection that had shaped her into the monster she'd become.

***

The next day, Lolita strode across the gym floor, her steps purposeful and precise. The familiar scent of chalk and sweat filled her nostrils, the air thick with the sounds of grunts and the slap of bodies against mats. She approached the uneven bars, her eyes narrowing as she calculated the routine in her mind. Each movement, each transition, mapped out with surgical precision. Error, mistakes—neither was permitted . . . perfection was the only acceptable outcome.

Lolita chalked her hands, the white powder forming a thin layer of armor against the unyielding metal. She mounted the bars with a fluid motion, her body flowing through the air like a lethal serpent. Muscles coiled and released, propelling her through handstands and release moves, defying gravity with each twist and turn.

Sweat beaded on her forehead, trickling down her face in rivulets. Her muscles screamed in protest, but Lolita pushed through the pain, her face a mask of stoic determination. Pain was a temporary inconvenience, a minor obstacle on the path to greatness. She would endure, she would conquer, she would prevail.

As she dismounted, sticking the landing with a resounding thud, a flash of movement caught her eye. Another gymnast, a mere mortal in this pantheon of demigods, approached with a tentative smile.

"Hey, Lolita! That was amazing. I was wondering if you'd like to grab a smoothie after practice, maybe chat about—"

Lolita cut her off with a withering glare, her voice as cold as the ice packs strapped to her aching joints. "I don't have time for idle chatter. If you want to be the best, you have to focus on your training, not silly distractions."

The girl recoiled as if slapped, her smile faltering. "I just thought—"

"You thought wrong." Lolita turned away, dismissing the girl with a flick of her wrist. "I'm here to win, not to make friends."

She stalked off, leaving the crestfallen gymnast in her wake. Lolita had no use for such weakness, for the soft emotions that clouded judgment and dulled the edge of ambition. She was a machine, honed and calibrated for a single purpose—victory at any cost.

Even if it meant giving up the comforts of a typical life, the temporary joys of companionship and solidarity, it would still be worth it. Lolita had her eyes on the prize, and nothing would stand in her way.

Not even her own humanity.

***

The memory of her father's face, warm and loving, intruded upon Lolita's thoughts as she made her way to the locker room. It was a rare moment, stolen from the relentless march of training and competition, a glimpse of the life she might have had if circumstances were different.

She was still aware of the comforting weight of his hand on her shoulder, could hear the pride in his voice as he spoke. "You're a marvel, my little Lolita. Watching you out there, it's like seeing poetry in motion."

Lolita had basked in his praise, a flower turning towards the sun. In that fleeting instant, the gym had melted away, the harsh fluorescent lights softening to a gentle glow. She was no longer Lolita, gymnastic prodigy and ruthless competitor. She was simply a daughter, cherished and adored.

But the moment was gone as quickly as it had come, her father's presence fading like a wisp of smoke. Lolita blinked, the memory dissipating as the locker room snapped back into focus. She couldn't afford to dwell on such sentimentality, not when the Olympic trials loomed on the horizon.

Shaking off the lingering warmth of her father's phantom embrace, Lolita began her pre-performance ritual. She methodically wrapped her wrists, the fabric a second skin against her flesh. She visualized her routine, each movement precise and perfect in her mind's eye.

As she slipped into her leotard, the material clinging to her slight frame, a flicker of something unfamiliar stirred in Lolita's chest. Nerves, perhaps? No, that was impossible. Lolita didn't get nervous; she was the one who made others tremble.

And yet, as she stepped out onto the mat, the weight of expectation settled heavy on her shoulders. The eyes of the judges, the crowd, her mother—they all bore into her, hungry for perfection, eager for the slightest misstep.

Lolita closed her eyes, drawing in a deep breath. She could do this. She was born for this moment, had sacrificed everything for the chance to prove herself on this stage.

As the first notes of her music filled the air, Lolita opened her eyes, a fierce determination burning in their depths. She would show them all what true greatness looked like.

And maybe, just maybe, she would make her father proud.

Lolita launched into her floor routine, her body a finely tuned instrument as she twisted and turned through the air. Each movement was a masterclass in control, her muscles coiling and releasing with the precision of a Swiss timepiece.

She could feel the energy of the crowd, their collective breath held. She opened with a double layout, landing with perfect control before flowing into her second tumbling pass—a round-off, back handspring into a full twisting double back. Her toes pointed, her lines perfect; she stuck each landing with the precision that had made her a favorite for Olympic trials. In the brief moments between elements, between the dance combinations that judges scrutinized as closely as the tumbling, she could feel the crowd's collective tension, their anticipation building as she prepared for her final pass—the round-off, back handspring, double pike that had become her signature. The pressure was immense, a tangible force pressing down on her shoulders, but Lolita refused to buckle under its weight.

From the corner of her eye, she glimpsed her mother, her face an unreadable mask as she tracked every move. There was no pride there, no hint of maternal affection—only a cold, clinical assessment of her daughter's performance.

As she prepared for her final pass, Lolita focused on the double pike—a move that had earned her countless accolades and the begrudging respect of her peers. She launched herself into the air, her body rotating with practiced precision.

But then, in a single, heart-stopping instant, everything changed. A searing pain shot through her knee, a white-hot agony that tore a scream from her throat. She sensed her control slipping away as she plummeted towards the mat.

The impact was brutal, a sickening crunch that echoed through the suddenly silent gym. Lolita lay there, her body twisted at an unnatural angle, her mind reeling as she tried to process what had just happened.

Around her, the world erupted into chaos—gasps of horror, the pounding of feet as coaches and medics rushed to her side. But Lolita barely registered any of it, her eyes fixed on the ceiling above, a single thought echoing through her mind:

> It's over. Everything I've worked for, everything I sacrificed—it's all gone.

As the pain washed over her in waves, a bitter laugh bubbled up in Lolita's throat. She had always prided herself on her control, on her ability to bend the world to her will. But in the end, even she was not immune to the cruel whims of fate.

***

Lolita lay on the mat, her face contorted in a mix of pain and disbelief. Her breath came in short, sharp gasps as she struggled to comprehend the magnitude of what had just happened. The searing agony in her knee was a constant reminder of the cruel twist of fate that had shattered her dreams in an instant.

Through the haze of pain, she saw her mother rushing towards her, pushing past the coaches and medics. Lolita had always seen her mother as an immovable force, a pillar of strength and determination. But now, as she knelt beside her fallen daughter, Lolita saw something she had never seen before: fear.

"Lolita, my darling," her mother whispered, her voice trembling. "It's going to be alright. We'll fix this, I promise."

But even as the words left her mother's lips, Lolita could see the doubt in her eyes. The disappointment. The realization that all their carefully laid plans had been undone by a single, devastating moment.

This is how failure feels, right? To have everything you've ever wanted ripped away from you?

As the EMTs performed tests on her knee, a wave of numbness washed over her. The pain had faded to a dull throb, overshadowed by the aching void that had opened up in her chest. The athletic trainer who had rushed to her side first was now helping secure the rigid splint, her face grim.

What am I supposed to do now? Who am I, if not Lolita Petrov, Olympic hopeful?

She had no answers, no clever quips or sharp retorts. For the first time in her life, Lolita was utterly lost, adrift in a sea of uncertainty.

As the doors of the ambulance closed behind her, Lolita closed her eyes, a single tear slipping down her cheek. She knew that this moment would define her, that it would shape the course of her life in ways she could not yet comprehend.

But one thing was certain: Lolita was not one to be broken. She would emerge stronger, more formidable. The world had not seen the last of her—of that, she was sure.

Chapter Two

Reinvention

B eads of sweat rolled down Lolita's sculpted abs as she cranked out another set of pull-ups, her grip never wavering on the chrome plated bar. The upscale Malibu gym was her temple, a place to hone both body and mind. She sensed the other patrons drinking in her flawless form, a mix of admiration and envy. Good. Let them stare. It would only make her next conquest that much easier.

Six months of physical therapy had taught Lolita one thing—bodies were machines that could be fixed, improved, controlled. While other patients complained and gave up, she studied and she challenged her therapist. She analyzed movements—hers and those around her—by watching how different bodies responded to different approaches. She interrogated her therapists about muscle groups, biomechanics, modalities, tissue healing, recovery processes. The mental part of healing was another favorite line of questioning . . .

Could we control ourselves and others by using our minds differently?

Most importantly, she learned how to systematize every-thing—tracking progress in spreadsheets, organizing exercises, documenting results.

Unable to train as a gymnast, she channeled her obsession with control into reshaping herself. The lean, graceful lines of her gymnast's body transformed into something more imposing. She built herself into a weapon—broad shoulders, sculpted biceps, the perpetually exposed abs that would become her trademark. If she couldn't command respect through Olympic medals, she'd command it through sheer physical presence.

When her physical therapist mentioned she'd make a good trainer, Lolita's mind turned. She started training at the gym in the evening while still attending UCLA during the day, testing her theories on willing subjects. Her methodical approach, born from years of gymnastics training, translated perfectly to personal training. Her detailed injury rehab spreadsheets evolved into a database to monitor every client's progress, developing systems to maximize results.

***

Dropping to the floor with feline grace, Lolita sauntered over to the rack of folded white towels. As she dabbed the sheen from her neck and chest, a middle-aged man in an expensive suit approached, clearing his throat awkwardly.

"Excuse me, are you Lolita? I hear you're the best personal trainer around."

She turned, eyeing him up and down with an appraising smirk. Prada loafers, Rolex watch, wedding ring. Typical executive with more money than willpower. Easy pickings.

*Another CEO who thinks his wallet can compensate
for his complete lack of athletic ability. Spoiler alert: it
can't, but I'll happily let him try to prove me wrong.*

"You heard right," Lolita said, cocking a hip. "The question is, can you handle my level of intensity? I don't coddle my clients."

"I'm no stranger to hard work. I built my tech company from the ground up."

"Is that so?" She stepped closer, trailing a finger along his silk tie. "Then you won't mind me saying your 'company' is looking a little . . . soft around the middle."

He blinked, mouth opening and closing like a landed fish. Lolita circled him slowly, her voice dripping with derision.

"What's the matter, big shot? Afraid to put your money where your mouth is?" She leaned in, hot breath tickling his ear. "Prove to me you've got what it takes. Sign up for my premium package, and I'll whip you into shape. Or are you all talk?"

The man swallowed hard, fumbling for his wallet. "Where do I sign?"

Lolita's smile was sharp as a blade. Another sucker, ready to be put through the wringer. She'd mold him like clay, pushing him to his limits and beyond. What was that saying all the bros were fond of, anyway?

Pain was merely weakness leaving the body.

As they discussed payment terms, Lolita's gaze flicked to the mirrored wall, catching sight of her own triumphant expression. This was her calling—bending others to her will, extracting every ounce of potential through sweat and tears. Her gymnastics background had given her an edge no certification program could match. She understood the body—and its predictable response—in a way few trainers did, and she could spot muscle imbalances and form issues that others missed. More importantly, she knew exactly how far she could push someone before they broke.

The tech mogul was just the first domino of the day. With each new victim, Lolita felt her power grow, an intoxicating rush no drug could match. Her client list had expanded rapidly, each success bringing more referrals, more desperate souls willing to pay premium rates for her particular brand of torture. She was making more in six months than most college graduates earned in a year.

Her mother had been furious when Lolita dropped out of UCLA.

"You're throwing everything away," her mother had screamed, pacing the sterile hospital room where Lolita lay, her knee swollen to twice its normal size. The doctor's words still echoed in her ears: torn ACL, MCL, extensive cartilage damage. Career-ending.

> *"There's nothing left to throw away," Lolita had replied, staring at the ceiling. "The scholarship was for gymnastics. Without that, UCLA is pointless."*

> *"So you'll just give up? Like a coward?" Natalya's voice dripped with disgust. "I didn't raise you to be weak."*

"No, Mother. You raised me to be perfect. And now that
I can't be perfect for you anymore, what's the point?"
The words hung between them like poison. Years passed
before they openly spoke again.

Lolita knew better. She didn't need a degree to command respect—she'd crafted something far more effective. The flashy biceps, the perpetually exposed abs, the cold, commanding presence—it all served to intimidate and control. Without traditional credentials, she'd built her reputation on results, and her growing waitlist proved her methods worked.

The tales of her training exploits were legendary in the LA gym scene.

Consider the hedge fund manager.

"Your form is sloppy," Lolita said, circling her newest client, who thought his wallet could compensate for weak discipline. She used the same cold, clinical tone her mother had once used on her. "Again."

The man's arms trembled as he attempted another set of pushups. Sweat darkened his designer workout gear.

"Is this the best you can do?" She crouched beside him, voice dripping with disappointment. "I thought you said you were serious about your fitness goals. Or was that just another empty promise, like the ones you make to your wife about working late?"

He glared at the personal dig. Lolita allowed herself a small smile—she'd done her research. She knew exactly where to press to make it hurt.

"I can do better," he panted.

"Prove it. Same time tomorrow. Don't disappoint me again."

Or the movie studio head of production.

"Remarkable progress," Lolita said, showing the newest ultra-wealthy whale his latest progress photos. Three months of carefully tracked measurements and annotated workout logs were spread across her desk. "You've exceeded every benchmark we set."

"Thanks to you," he beamed, clearly proud. "My wife can't believe the transformation."

"Imagine what we could achieve in six more months." Lolita pulled out a new contract. "I've designed a specialized program just for you. Exclusive access, personalized nutrition, 24/7 availability." She named a price that made him flinch.

"That's . . . steep."

"Is it?" She pulled up his before photos. "Look at what you were before me. Weak. Soft. Now you're becoming something extraordinary." She paused. "Of course, if you'd rather return to that version of yourself . . ."

He signed without further hesitation. Lolita filed away the contract, knowing she'd just secured another perfectly dependent client. Her mother had used fear to control her. Lolita had learned to use pride instead—much more effective, and far more difficult to break free from.

The myth was real; she could get results, and she could bend others to her will.

***

Within six months of dropping out, Lolita had transformed the gym's training program. Her client files were meticulously organized, color-coded by goals and progress. She'd developed a proprietary system for tracking measurements, nutrition, and progress photos. Other trainers started asking to use her methods, but she kept them to herself. Control was power, after all.

Her reputation grew beyond just getting results. Wealthy clients appreciated her attention to detail, her ability to systematize every aspect of their fitness journey. She wasn't just training bodies—she was creating a machine of efficiency and results.

As Lolita finalized the details with her newest client, a figure caught her eye from across the gym floor. At first glance, he seemed unremarkable—just another middle-aged man with a slight paunch and thinning hair. But something about his presence commanded attention, an aura of quiet authority that set him apart from the preening peacocks and desperate housewives.

He moved with a purposeful stride, eyes scanning the room like a general surveying his troops. When his gaze locked with Lolita's, a jolt of recognition passed between them. Here was a kindred spirit, someone who understood the thrill of the hunt and the rush of conquest.

Lolita excused herself from a new mark, leaving him to fumble with the contract. She sauntered across the gym, hips swaying like a metronome. As she drew closer, the man's features came into sharp focus—a firm jaw, piercing blue eyes, and a smile that promised both danger and delight.

"I don't believe we've met," Lolita said, extending a hand. "Lolita, personal trainer extraordinaire."

The man took her hand in a firm grip, his skin warm and slightly calloused. "Tony. I've heard great things about you. Your reputation precedes you."

Lolita arched an eyebrow. "All good, I hope?"

Tony chuckled, a low rumble in his chest. "Depends on your definition of good. From what I hear, you're a force to be reckoned with. A woman who knows what she wants and isn't afraid to take it.

"I've been watching how you operate. The way you organize everything, create systems, maintain control. It's impressive."

Lolita raised an eyebrow. "I'm sensing this isn't about personal training."

"Several years ago, I started a company, Cum As You Are—we're small now, but we have potential. What we lack is organization, discipline, someone who understands how to maximize efficiency." He paused, studying her reaction. "Right now, we're chaos. But with the right person implementing the right systems . . ."

"And you think I'm that person?" Lolita asked, intrigued despite herself.

"I think you understand something fundamental that most people don't—control isn't just about force. It's about creating systems that make people want to fall in line. I've seen how your clients practically beg to follow your rules." He smiled. "Imagine applying that on a larger scale."

Tony reached into his pocket, producing a sleek black business card. He pressed it into Lolita's palm, his fingers lingering just a moment too long.

"Stop by my office. I have a feeling this could blossom into a beautiful partnership."

With a final nod, Tony turned and strode away, leaving Lolita clutching the card like a lifeline. She didn't know what the future held, but one thing was certain—her days as a mere personal trainer were numbered. She knew a little about Cum As You Are—CAYA to locals—a small *film* company. This chance meeting with Tony had the potential to open the door to a whole new world, and she was ready to step through it, no matter the cost.

As Lolita walked back to the locker room, she could feel the weight of the business card in her pocket. A smile crept across her face. Adult entertainment was unprepared for what followed.

***

Lolita stood in her minimalist apartment, Tony's business card pinched between her sculpted fingers. She turned it over, examining the embossed logo—a sleek, stylized *V* that seemed to hold a thousand promises.

Her mind raced with possibilities. What could someone like Tony propose? She knew his reputation, of course. Everyone in LA did. Cum As You Are—though small by comparison—was an up-and-coming adult entertainment empire on the West Coast, and Tony was a man with the power to make or break careers with a snap of his fingers.

Lolita's lips curved into a smirk. She'd always been ambitious, hungry for success. And now, opportunity was knocking—or rather, slipping its business card into her hand with a knowing smile.

She tapped the card against her chin, weighing her options. On one hand, her personal training business was thriving. She had a steady stream of wealthy clients, each one willing to pay top dollar for her unique blend of tough love and cutting wit. It was a comfortable life, one she'd built through sheer determination and an unwavering commitment to her own success.

But comfort was for the weak. Lolita craved power, the kind that came from being at the top of the food chain. And something told her that Tony could give her that power, if she was willing to take the leap.

Her decision made, Lolita reached for her phone. She dialed the number on the card, her fingers steady and sure.

"CAYA Productions, this is Andrea, how may I help you?" a clipped voice answered.

"This is Lolita," she said, her tone dripping with confidence. "I believe Tony is expecting my call."

"One moment."

"Lolita." Tony's voice oozed through the phone, rich and smooth as honey. "I'm so glad you called."

"Well, when a man like you makes an invitation, it's hard to refuse," she said, her words laced with innuendo.

"I had a feeling you were a woman who recognized opportunity when she saw it," Tony chuckled. "So, what do you say? Stop by the studio offices tomorrow afternoon? We can discuss the details of my little proposition."

Lolita's heart raced with anticipation. This was it—the moment that would change everything.

"I wouldn't miss it for the world," she said.

As she hung up the phone, Lolita allowed herself a moment of triumph. She'd always known she was destined for greater things, and now fate had delivered her the perfect opportunity.

***

The sun was relentless as Lolita stepped out of the apartment, her sculpted body gleaming with sweat under its intense heat. She slid into her new Corvette, putting the top down and revving the engine. The roar of the engine was a symphony to her ears, a celebration of her absolute control.

As she sped through the Malibu canyons, Lolita allowed herself a
rare smile. Let her mother rage about wasted potential. She'd found
her true calling, and her transformation was complete. Gone was the
mousy, bookish girl. In her place stood a force of nature, an Ama-
zon warrior in heels. Her coiffed blonde hair, now spiky and defiant,
framed a face chiseled by countless hours of rigorous exercise. Every
muscle was etched in definition, her body a living, breathing adver-
tisement for her ruthless workout regime.

***

The Malibu Pier stretched into the Pacific like a weathered sentinel, its
wooden planks bearing silent witness to decades of California history.
Originally built in 1905 for shipping agricultural goods, the 780-foot
structure had evolved into something far more iconic—a symbol of
Southern California's endless summer and the birthplace of modern
surf culture.

Lolita stood at the pier's entrance—where she had gazed longingly
years ago—watching surfers carve through the legendary three-point
break at Surfrider Beach. The waves here had drawn everyone from
local legends to Hollywood starlets, the same water that once carried
farm goods now delivering rides stretching 300 yards or more.

The pier had survived war—serving as a Coast Guard lookout sta-
tion in the 1940s—and nature's fury, closing for over a decade after
devastating storms in the late 1990s. Now restored to its former glory,
it stood as a testament to resilience and reinvention. Something about
that resonated with Lolita as she prepared for her meeting with Tony.

The salt-laden breeze whipped at her hair as she walked to the end,
watching the surfers below, their graceful movements reminiscent of

her own long-ago routines on the balance beam. But she wasn't here to reminisce. She was here to remind herself that even the most iconic institutions could be transformed into something new, something powerful. Something controlled.

Lolita turned from the pier's weathered railing, taking in the sweeping view of the Malibu coast. The hills rose dramatically from the shoreline, their drought-golden slopes dotted with scrub brush and scattered eucalyptus trees. Modern homes perched precariously on the cliffs, a testament to humanity's determination to claim even the most challenging terrain.

Her eyes fixed on the tan-colored building nestled at the base of those hills, its clean lines and expansive windows a stark contrast to the pier's rustic charm. Tony's office. Her future. The short walk along the beach would take her from this relic of old California to what she hoped would be her gateway to power.

She made her way down the pier's wooden planks, her heels clicking purposefully against the bleached boards. Her six-foot-four frame commanded attention as she strode past the fishing families and photo-snapping tourists, who openly gaped at the force of nature in their midst. Some pretended not to stare, casting furtive glances over their shoulders. Others made no attempt to hide their fascination with her sculpted physique and predatory grace. Lolita drank in their attention like a fine wine, each stunned look and whispered comment feeding her sense of power. She'd come a long way from her humble beginnings, clawing her way to the top through sheer determination and ruthlessness.

At the pier's entrance, she turned right, her long legs carrying her effortlessly across the damp sand toward the tan building. The ocean breeze carried the scent of salt and ambition, and Lolita allowed herself a small smile. By sunset, everything would change.

***

Tucked away in a strip mall across from the pier, Lolita spied the small office. As she'd learned from her research after meeting him, Tony was a notorious, up-and-coming figure in the adult entertainment world. The rumors didn't do him justice. He oozed power and charisma, his presence commanding the room.

As their eyes met, a shiver of anticipation raced down Lolita's spine. She'd heard whispers of his small studio and their propensity for bending a few—several?—rules. The more she'd learned about the industry, the more she recognized its potential. Here was a world built on desperation and shattered dreams, where vulnerable people would do anything for a shot at success. Her mind raced with possibilities—contracts designed to create dependency, living arrangements that enabled constant surveillance, systematic isolation masked as "exclusive representation." She could craft a perfect system of control, one that would make her gymnastics coaches look amateur in comparison. In this world, she wouldn't just shape bodies like she had as a trainer—she would shape destinies.

Lolita cared little about the suffering of others. All that mattered was she was about to play in the big leagues—and she always won.

Striding over, she extended a manicured hand, her lipsticked smile as sharp as a knife's edge. "Tony, darling. I've heard so much about you."

And with those words, Lolita, the newest and most formidable player in the world of adult entertainment, was born. Determined to claw her way to the top, no matter the cost, she would stop at nothing to reshape the industry in her image. And those who stood in her way? They'd soon learn a valuable lesson:

Cross Lolita at your own peril.

Chapter Three

The Rise

The Corvette glided to a stop at the entrance of the Cum As You Are studios, a short distance up the coast from the Malibu office. A long, slender leg emerged, the stiletto heel striking the pavement with crisp authority. Lolita unfolded herself from the low sports car, her icy blue eyes immediately scanning the perimeter like a hawk surveying its hunting grounds. She frowned, noticing the lackadaisical posture of the gate guard. Amateur hour, she thought wryly. Tony may be a visionary, but his security protocols were woefully lacking. She made a mental note to overhaul the entire system at the first opportunity.

Striding through the gates, her lithe, sculpted figure drew appreciative glances from the few employees milling about. Lolita paid them no heed, her mind already cataloging the disorganized bustle of activity around her. Racks of skimpy costumes were haphazardly pushed against walls, tangled cords snaked underfoot, and harried production assistants scurried by clutching overstuffed binders. It was like watching a colony of ants that had gotten into the sugar bowl—frenzied, chaotic, and in desperate need of discipline.

"Lolita!" a young man called out, hurrying toward her. "I didn't expect you so early. I thought Tony said—"

Lolita silenced him with a single arched eyebrow. "Tony doesn't dictate my schedule," she said coolly. "And from the looks of things, that's a good thing. This place is running like a two-bit strip club in Reno."

The assistant blanched, his cheap tie bobbing as he swallowed nervously. "We've been a bit understaffed, and the shooting schedule has been—"

"Save it," Lolita cut him off with a dismissive wave. "I don't have time for excuses." She swept past him, her mind already whirring with ruthless efficiency. Staffing, schedules, security—it would all need to be overhauled and brought to heel under her unyielding control. In this dazzling fantasy fortress, chaos and weakness had no place. Only cold, hard perfection would do. And Lolita would make damn sure that's exactly what Tony got.

The transition from controlling bodies to controlling souls happened gradually, then all at once. Tony's offer came at the perfect moment—Lolita had already begun to tire of mere physical dominance. She spent six months studying the adult entertainment industry, learning its pressure points and vulnerabilities.

By the time she implemented her first systems at the studio, she had already mapped out how to transform their small operation into an empire of absolute control.

***

Lolita moved with predatory grace into the bustling production area, her icy gaze sweeping over the assembled employees like a predator sizing up its prey. A group of actors huddled near the craft services table, their nervous chatter falling silent as she approached.

"Well, well," Lolita said, her voice as smooth as silk and twice as dangerous. "If it isn't the talent. Tell me, darlings, how are you finding your accommodations? Comfortable? Satisfying?" Her eyes glinted with a challenge, daring them to voice a complaint.

A petite brunette stepped forward, her hands twisting anxiously. "Actually, Lolita, some of us were wondering about the new contract terms. The exclusivity clause seems a bit—"

"Generous?" Lolita finished, her smile razor-sharp. "My dear, you're not here to think. You're here to perform. And if you can't appreciate the opportunity we're giving you, well . . ." She let the threat hang in the air, heavy and oppressive.

The girl swallowed hard, her face paling. "No, I . . . I understand. Thank you, Lolita."

"Excellent." Lolita turned to the rest of the group, her gaze hardening. "Cum As You Are is not just a job. It's a privilege. And privileges can be revoked." With that, she spun on her heel and stalked away, leaving a wake of fear and submission behind her.

As she navigated the labyrinthine halls of the compound, Lolita's mind raced with plans and contingencies. Tony might be the face of the company, but she was its backbone—the steel beneath the silk. And she would not rest until every last cog in this machine was turning in perfect, obedient synchronicity.

***

She reached Tony's office and entered without knocking, her presence commanding immediate attention. Tony looked up from his desk, his expression a mix of annoyance and grudging respect.

"Lolita," he greeted, leaning back in his chair. "To what do I owe the pleasure of this interruption?"

"We need to talk about the state of this operation. The security is laughable, the staff is undisciplined, and the talent is getting restless. And though it's bigger than the site we had years ago, we're running out of room."

Tony's eyes narrowed. "I didn't realize you were gunning for my job, Lolita. Last I checked, I was still the one signing your paychecks."

She just stared at him.

"Fine. What do you suggest?"

Lolita smiled, a cat with a canary. "I thought you'd never ask." She pulled out a notebook and began outlining her vision—a well-oiled machine of control, efficiency, and unquestioned obedience. Buildings. Offices. Security. A sanctuary to accomplish all they dreamed of. Each word shaped the future of Cum As You Are; dark and glittering and utterly, utterly ruthless.

***

Later that night, alone in her office, Lolita replayed her harsh words to the young actress. "If you can't appreciate the opportunity we're giving you . . ." The phrase hung in the air, and suddenly she heard it—her mother's voice coming from her own lips. The same cutting tone, the same cruel manipulation wrapped in the guise of "opportunity."

She caught her reflection in the window, her sculpted form rigid with tension. For a moment, she saw her mother standing there instead—tall, unyielding, demanding perfection at any cost. Lolita's hand trembled slightly as she reached for her glass of water.

"I'm nothing like her," she said to her reflection. But the words rang hollow, and she knew—deep in the marrow of her bones—that she had become exactly what she'd once despised. She had transformed her mother's obsession with physical perfection into something perhaps even more insidious: the ruthless pursuit of absolute control over others.

The realization should have horrified her. Instead, she felt a grim satisfaction. At least she was better at it than her mother had ever been.

***

"I think I've found it," Tony said, spreading architectural drawings across his desk. His eyes gleamed with barely contained excitement. "An old estate in the Malibu hills. The previous owner went bankrupt, trying to build some sort of wellness retreat. There's already a main building, several smaller structures, and enough land to expand. Best part? It's isolated. No nosy neighbors, no prying eyes."

Lolita studied the plot, her mind already calculating possibilities. The layout was perfect—a blank canvas waiting to be transformed by her exacting vision. The Malibu hills' sprawling expanse would serve as their secluded fortress, close enough to Hollywood for industry connections. A stunning mid-century modern home, the crown jewel of the property, boasted clean lines, glass walls, and dramatic angles that seemed to float above the Pacific. This architectural masterpiece would become their headquarters, finally bringing their scattered operations under one roof. The rest of the former wellness retreat offered everything else they needed—auxiliary buildings perfect for production, and enough land to expand. Behind imposing gates, it would become a world of its own—a self-contained sanctuary where the normal rules of society ceased to exist. She could already envision the security checkpoints, the controlled access, the carefully monitored boundaries, and, most importantly, the residential complex where their "talent" would live under constant surveillance.

With the plans spread across Lolita's desk, covered in her precise annotations. What others saw as just another building, she envisioned as a masterpiece of control.

"Individual rooms, each with their own surveillance feed," she explained to Tony. "Key card access, monitored entry and exit points. We'll call it 'luxury accommodation'—a perk of signing with us exclusively."

"Sounds expensive," Tony noted.

"An investment," Lolita corrected. "We charge them for the privilege, of course. Room and board, security fees, facility maintenance. By the time they realize they're in debt to us, it'll be too late." She traced a finger along the planned security checkpoints. "The best prisons are the ones where the inmates think they're free."

"When can we start construction?" she asked, her lips curving into a predatory smile. This wasn't just a property acquisition; it was the foundation of an empire.

***

Lolita wasted no time putting her plans into action. With a cold efficiency that bordered on the inhuman, she set about transforming their new compound into a fortress of her own design. Security cameras sprouted like weeds, their unblinking eyes covering every inch of the property. Access codes and biometric scans became the new keys to the kingdom, and woe to any employee who dared to forget them.

Were these to keep people out . . . or to keep people in?

As she watched her protocols fall into place, Lolita allowed herself a small smile of satisfaction. This world, hers now, operated on precision; every step planned, every detail accounted for. She reveled in power, but a quiet question persisted.

For how long?

***

She noticed the girl right away—fresh-faced, barely twenty, with a mix of ambition and naivety that made her perfect prey. The actress had just finished her third shoot, riding high on the attention and the biggest paycheck she'd ever seen. But Lolita recognized the subtle signs of doubt creeping in, the way her smile faltered when she thought no one was watching.

"You're different from the others," Lolita said, cornering her in the dressing room with practiced casualness. "I see real star potential in you." She kept her voice warm, maternal almost—a stark contrast to her usual icy demeanor. "But this industry can chew you up if you don't have the right guidance. The right protection." Lolita watched the girl's expression carefully, noting how she leaned forward, hungry for validation. "I could help you navigate it. Make sure you get the best roles, the best rates. Keep you safe from the . . . seedier elements."

Lolita gestured to the luxurious surroundings of the newly built compound. "We take care of our own here. Full medical, security, housing—all the perks of an actual career." She let that sink in before adding the hook: "Of course, that would require an exclusive contract. But isn't your future worth it?"

The girl hesitated, and Lolita felt the familiar thrill of the hunt. This was what she lived for—the delicate art of breaking someone's will while creating the illusion of choice. She'd learned long ago that true control wasn't about brute force; it was about understanding people's fears, their desperate need to belong, to feel special.

She pulled out her phone, scrolling through photos with practiced indifference. "Remember Carmen? Thought she could make it on her own?" She showed the girl a carefully curated image—one of their former actresses, now clearly struggling. "Last I heard, she was doing bachelor parties in Vegas. Such a waste." Lolita shook her head with manufactured concern. "But you? You could be different. You could be a star."

She watched the fear bloom in the girl's eyes, followed quickly by desperate hope. It was a dance Lolita had perfected—the careful balance of threat and promise, stick and carrot, fear and ambition. Every gesture, every word, was choreographed to perfection, just like her old gymnastics routines. But this performance brought a different satisfaction. Here, she wasn't just executing moves; she was pulling strings, molding minds, crafting dependencies with surgical precision.

The papers were signed that afternoon, the girl never realizing she'd just agreed to terms that would make it nearly impossible to leave. Lolita suppressed a smile as she watched the pen move across the page. The "housing fees" would accumulate faster than they could be paid off—a system she'd designed herself. An exclusive contract would prevent her from working elsewhere. The "image consultation" sessions would progressively strip away her identity, replacing it with whatever persona the studio required. By the time she understood the trap—the mounting debt, the contract clauses that kept her bound to the studio, the carefully orchestrated dependency—it would be too late.

As Lolita filed away the contract, she noted the girl's name for future reference. Another asset secured, another soul under her perfect control. This was where she excelled—not just controlling bodies like in her training days, but controlling minds, destinies, entire lives. It was nothing personal, she reassured herself. Purely business. And in this business, control was everything. After all, hadn't her mother taught her that perfection required sacrifice? She was handing down that lesson, one broken spirit at a time.

***

A subtle movement on a front gate motion detector caught Lolita's eye—something the guards had missed. She leaned forward and quickly switched her focus to Monitor 3, studying the couple approaching the gate. Their clothes were expensive but slightly wrinkled, their body language tense but practiced. The woman's hand kept straying to her purse.

"Thompson," Lolita said into her radio. "Your 2 o'clock. Notice anything odd about our visitors?"

The guard's voice crackled back. "Just looks like another angry parent . . ."

"Look closer," she cut him off. "The man's right hand keeps twitching toward his pocket. The woman's wearing shoes she can run in with that designer dress. And there's a van idling just beyond the camera's range."

She watched the guard straighten up as he processed her observations. The couple reached the gate, their practiced speeches beginning: "That's my daughter in there! Ava! AVA!" Their voices cracked with desperation.

"Now you see it, don't you?" Lolita's voice was bitter. "This isn't a spontaneous visit. They planned this. Probably have someone waiting to help with an extraction." She stood, fingers drumming on her desk. "Call in the second team. Watch the perimeter. And Thompson? Next time, I expect you to spot these things before I do."

As security mobilized with synchronized precision, Lolita allowed herself a small smile. They were learning. But more importantly, they were learning to see the world through her eyes—where every detail could signal a threat to her perfect system of control.

Lolita's jaw clenched. She recognized the name they shouted—one of their newer acquisitions, barely nineteen. The girl had signed an ironclad contract, legally an adult. But watching her parents pound against the gate, something twisted in Lolita's gut.

She picked up her phone. "Increase Ava's supervision. No phone privileges, no internet access."

As the security teams escorted the couple away, their cries echoing through the compound, Lolita caught sight of Ava watching from her window. The girl's face was blank, emotionless—a perfect mirror of what Lolita had become.

Later that night, Lolita gathered the *house mothers* around a holographic display of the compound. "Starting today, every resident's movements will be tracked through their ID badges. Green means they're where they should be. Yellow means they've deviated from schedule. Red . . ." she paused, letting her gaze sweep the room, "means we have a problem."

She demonstrated by moving a test badge through different zones. "The system automatically logs everything—time stamps, duration, unauthorized interactions. If someone lingers too long in restricted areas or meets with unapproved visitors, we'll know."

Sandra, the newest *house mother*, raised her hand timidly. "Isn't this a bit . . . extreme?"

Lolita's smile didn't reach her eyes. "What's extreme is how much money we lose when talent goes rogue. This protects our investment. And them."

***

The control room was a hive of activity as Lolita strode in, her presence commanding immediate attention. Dozens of screens flickered with live feeds from every corner of the compound, a testament to the ever-watchful eye of her security systems.

"Status report," she barked, her gaze sweeping over the assembled technicians.

"All systems are green," one of them said, his fingers flying over the keyboard. "We've got eyes on every inch of the perimeter, and the new motion sensors are online."

Lolita nodded, a flicker of satisfaction crossing her features. "Good. And the access controls?"

"Upgraded and fully operational. No one gets in or out without our say-so."

A smile curved Lolita's lips, sharp and predatory. "Excellent."

She moved closer to the screens, her eyes drinking in the details. Every camera, every sensor, every lock and key—all of it was under her control. And control was everything. Her gaze lingered on the feed from Justine's room, now empty and silent. A reminder of the one piece that had slipped through her grasp.

But not for long.

"Keep me updated on any developments," Lolita said, turning to leave. "And if anyone so much as breathes in a way that seems off, I want to know about it."

The technicians nodded, a chorus of "Yes, ma'am" following her out the door.

Lolita's heels clicked against the polished floor as she made her way through the compound, her mind already churning with contingency plans and worst-case scenarios. She was so lost in thought that she almost didn't notice Tony until he was right in front of her, his expression an odd mix of amusement and wariness.

"I hear you've been busy."

Lolita shrugged, a calculated gesture of nonchalance. "Just doing my job."

Tony chuckled, the sound low and rich. "And then some. The way I hear it, you've got this place locked down tighter than Fort Knox."

Lolita's lips twitched, a hint of a smile tugging at the corners. "Well, someone has to keep things running smoothly around here."

"And you're doing a hell of a job," Tony said, his tone turning serious. "Which is why I want to make it official."

"Official?"

"You've been my right hand for a while," Tony said, his gaze steady on hers. "My most trusted advisor. There's no one else I'd rather have by my side. I'd like you to be the Cum As You Are COO."

For a moment, Lolita simply stared at him, her expression unreadable. A smile crept across her face—genuine this time, with an edge of
triumph.

"I'm honored," she said, reaching out to shake his hand. "And I
won't let you down."

Tony grinned, his grip firm and strong. "I know you won't."

As they continued down the hallway together, Lolita felt a surge
of satisfaction wash over her. Everything was falling into place, just as
she'd planned.

And with Tony's support, there was nothing that could stop her
now.

***

Lolita settled into her office chair, the leather creaking softly beneath
her. The day's events played through her mind like a highlight reel,
each success fueling her growing sense of invincibility.

She reached for her laptop, clicking through the compound's security feeds with practiced efficiency. Every camera, every sensor, every
lock—all under her watchful eye. A symphony of control, orchestrated by her own hand.

As she basked in the glow of her own success, a small voice whispered in the back of her mind. A warning, a reminder that pride comes
before the fall.

But Lolita brushed it aside, her confidence unwavering. She'd
worked too hard, come too far, to let doubt creep in now. The challenges ahead were simply opportunities for her to prove her worth, to
cement her place at the top of the food chain. Her eyes glinted with
anticipation.

Bring it on. I'm ready for whatever comes next.

And with that, Lolita turned her attention back to her work, plotting her next moves with the precision and ruthlessness that had gotten her this far. The game was far from over—but as far as she was concerned, victory was already hers for the taking.

Chapter Four

The Foundation Cracks

The glittering ballroom buzzed with energy, the crème de la crème of the adult entertainment industry mingling beneath the shimmering chandeliers. Lolita stood at the edge of the crowd, her eyes scanning the room with calculated precision.

And then she saw her.

Across the sea of designer gowns and tailored suits, a shock of flaming red hair caught Lolita's attention. The woman moved through the crowd with a grace that seemed almost out of place in this den of sin and debauchery, her head held high, her eyes sparkling with a fierce determination.

Lolita felt a flicker of spite, a tug of anger that she doubted she'd ever forget. She watched as the redhead navigated the room, her smile sharp and her wit even sharper as she charmed the industry bigwigs with effortless ease.

But beneath the polished exterior, Lolita sensed something else. A resilience. A strength forged in the fires of adversity. She survived; a kindred spirit resisting those who tried to break her.

And yet, as Lolita studied her, an inexplicable unease coiled in her gut. There was something about this woman, something that set her apart from the rest of the vapid, eager-to-please starlets that populated these events.

Years ago, she signed a young actress to a contract that she thought was impossible to break. An agreement nobody could ever break free from. This one did. This one slipped away.

Lolita's instincts, honed by years of navigating treacherous waters, whispered a warning. This woman was not to be underestimated. She was a wild card, an unknown variable in the carefully controlled equation of Lolita's world.

As the redhead's gaze met hers across the room, Lolita felt a crackle of electricity, a silent acknowledgment passing between them. In that moment, she knew their paths would cross tonight, for better or for worse.

Lolita's lips curled into a smile, a challenge glinting in her eyes. Let the games begin, she thought, as she raised her champagne glass in a silent toast to the woman who had captured her attention so completely.

In this glittering world of illusions and deceit, had Lolita finally met her match?

Never.

***

Lolita's abs rippled beneath her fitted black dress as she sauntered over to the redhead, a predatory gleam in her eyes. Time to pour on the charm. "Well, well, if it isn't the big star herself," she said, her voice dripping with equal parts honey and venom. "When we first met, I thought we'd never lose you, Justine. It's so good to see you."

Justine met her gaze, a smirk playing at the corners of her mouth. "Lolita, I'm *so* glad you're here. I hope you are doing well," she said, her tone laced with a sarcastic edge.

"Always," Lolita countered, her smile razor-sharp.

"Are you though?" Justine stepped closer, her voice dropping to just above a whisper. "Tell me, do you still check the security feeds at 3am? Do you lie awake wondering which one of your perfectly controlled puppets will break free next? That's the thing about cages, Lolita—eventually, they all develop cracks."

Lolita fought to maintain her composure, but something in Justine's words hit too close to home. This wasn't just another rebellious performer—Justine understood the system because she'd escaped it.

"You know nothing about what we've built here," Lolita hissed.

"I know everything," Justine said calmly. "The fake contracts. The mysterious disappearances. The *medical emergencies*. How many people are you willing to sacrifice before it all comes crashing down?" She paused, her eyes glittering with satisfaction. "By the way, how's your mother? Still pushing for perfection at any cost?"

The mention of her mother sent an icy spike through Lolita's chest; Justine's words had already done their damage. So she responded in the only way she knew. She laughed, low and dangerous. "Sharp as a tack, aren't you? I remember that." She leaned in closer, her breath ghosting over Justine's ear. "I just wanted to invite you personally to return to our little Cum As You Are family. I hope to work with you again soon."

Justine met her gaze, unfazed by the invasion of her personal space. "Is that a promise or a threat?"

Before Lolita could respond, Justine continued,

"You're always controlling everything, aren't you, Lolita?" Justine's eyes glittered with knowing malice. "But control is just an illusion. You, of all people, should understand that. One wrong move, one slip on the beam . . . and everything crashes down."

The words hit Lolita like a physical blow. How did Justine know about her gymnastics career? About the injury that had shattered her Olympic dreams?

"You're not the only one who knows how to gather information," Justine continued, her voice low. "Everything you've built here—it's all balanced on a knife's edge. Just like you were, right before you fell."

Lolita felt genuine shock for the first time in years. Not just by Justine's words, but by the truth behind them. She'd spent so long crafting her perfect system of control, she'd forgotten how quickly it could all fall apart.

Before she could digest all she'd heard, a commotion erupted from across the room. A group of people had gathered around a prone figure on the floor, whispers of "overdose" rippling through the crowd.

The delicate crystal champagne flute in Lolita's hand trembled, threatening to shatter as shouts and crashes exploded around her. Through the sea of designer gowns and tuxedos, she saw Alex crumpled on the marble floor, her skin an unnatural shade of gray, lips tinged blue. One of their top performers, their *golden girl*, now nothing more than a liability sprawled across the floor of Hollywood's most exclusive industry event.

"Nobody touch her!" Lolita's voice cut through the panicked murmurs as she strode over, her heels clicking like a judge's gavel. She knelt beside Alex, careful to keep her designer dress from touching the floor.

Her pulse was a thin, weak thread against her skin; each shallow breath hitched and strained. Mascara-stained tears had left black tracks down her cheeks, and a fine powder residue dusted her nostrils. Amateur. Sloppy.

She took a moment to glance at the partygoers and caught Justine's knowing gaze from across the room; Lolita couldn't shake the feeling that the cracks in her carefully constructed facade were showing.

"Get her out of here. Now." Lolita's command mobilized their security team instantly. She watched as they lifted Alex with practiced efficiency—they'd done this before, though never quite so publicly. As they carried her away, Lolita glimpsed track marks on Alex's arm, poorly concealed by makeup. How had she missed the signs?

Hours later, after the damage control and carefully crafted press statements, Lolita sat in her office reviewing Alex's file. The signs had been there: missed shoots, erratic behavior, desperate requests for payment advances. But she'd ignored them, too focused on the profit margins Alex brought in. Now it was all going to hell.

Her phone buzzed—a text from the private clinic where they'd taken Alex.

She's stable. But she's talking. Asking for a lawyer.

Lolita's fingers tightened around her phone. One weak link could bring down their entire empire. She thought of Justine's knowing smirk from across the ballroom earlier, of the whispers already spreading through the industry. The foundation was cracking, and for the first time in years, Lolita felt something dangerously close to fear.

She pressed a button on her intercom. "Get me everything we have on Alex. Family, friends, debts—everything." Her voice was steel, cold and unyielding. "And call Tony. We need to discuss contingency plans."

As she hung up, Lolita caught her reflection in the window. Her face was a mask of control, but her eyes betrayed the truth—things were unraveling. Alex wasn't just an overdose; she was a symptom of a deeper rot, one that threatened to expose everything they'd built.

And Lolita knew, with chilling certainty, that she would do whatever it took to keep that from happening.

***

Lolita paced in her office, her mind churning as she tried to rationalize the incident with Alex. "Just a minor hiccup," she whispered to herself, the words laced with sarcasm, like a poison she couldn't quite swallow. "Nothing a little damage control can't fix."

But even as the words left her lips, she was aware of a nagging doubt creeping in. How many more "hiccups" could they afford before the entire empire came crashing down? She glanced at the surveillance monitors, the flickering images of the compound suddenly seeming more like a prison than a palace.

"No," she said, slamming her fist on the desk. "We've come too far to let one weak link bring us down." She straightened her shoulders, her sculpted abs rippling beneath her form-fitting top. "Our systems are effective. Necessary. We just need to tighten the reins a little more."

With a deep breath, Lolita strode out of her office. She had a show to put on.

***

The performers gathered in the sleek, modern auditorium, an undercurrent of tension palpable in the air. Lolita took the stage, her presence commanding instant attention.

"I'm sure you've all heard about the incident with Alex," she began, her tone light and nonchalant. "Just a little too much partying, nothing to worry about. She'll return to set in no time."

She surveyed the room, her sharp gaze daring anyone to challenge her. "Let this serve as a reminder for each of you. We have a reputation to uphold, and we can't afford any slip-ups. You're here because you're the best of the best, and I expect nothing less than perfection."

Lolita paused, letting her words sink in. "Remember, you're not just performers. You're part of something bigger. Cum As You Are isn't just a company; it's a lifestyle. A family. And we take care of our own."

She paused for effect and flashed a smile, but it didn't quite reach her eyes. "Now, let's get back to work. We've got content to create and an industry to dominate."

As the performers dispersed, Lolita felt a flicker of unease. She had delivered her words perfectly, but the cracks in her confidence were growing harder to ignore. How long could she keep up this charade before the truth came crashing down around her?

***

Lolita returned to her office, the unsettling meeting with the actors still on her mind. They had every reason to demand answers. Rumors were swirling about Cum As You Are's practices, the whispers growing louder by the day.

She paced the spacious room, her ever-present heels striking the marble floor. Tony's voice echoed in her head, a constant refrain: "Control your image or they'll control you, Lolita. Perception is everything."

With a sigh, she sat down at her desk. The glowing screen of her computer taunted her, a reminder of the empire she was struggling to protect. With a few keystrokes, she could access footage from any set or a dossier on any performer.

Lolita's fingers hovered over the keys; then she stopped. No, she thought. I can't afford to show weakness. Not now. Instead, she poured a drink, the icy fizz of the sparkling water a stark contrast to the stale, dry air of the office. "To the art of illusion," she toasted, then downed the entire glass in one go.

Lolita knew the truth better than anyone: an empire built on secrets and lies was bound to crumble. But not on her watch, she swore. No, she would do anything to protect what they'd built—even if it meant becoming the very monster she'd once sworn to destroy.

***

The next day, Lolita entered the production building, her icy demeanor securely in place. She wove through the bustling soundstages, nodding curtly at the performers and staff who scurried out of her path.

In the conference room, the *house mothers* waited, tension heavy in the air. Lolita took her seat at the head of the table, her expression impassive.

"Ladies," Lolita said, surveying the anxious faces before her. "I see we're all dressed for a funeral. How fitting, considering someone's career is about to die if this happens again."

Murmurs rippled through the room, but Lolita silenced them with a look. "Yes, yes, I know about the . . . incident." She waved her manicured hand dismissively. "Rest assured, it won't happen again."

The *house mothers* exchanged skeptical glances, but none dared voice their doubts aloud.

Lolita leaned forward, her eyes cold. "I don't care what you have to do, but I expect each of you to tighten the reins on your girls. We cannot afford another slip-up. Understood?"

A mumbling chorus of "Yes, Lolita" filled the room. But she wasn't finished.

"Good," she said, "because the second this becomes a problem, I cannot . . . manage . . . I will not hesitate to take care of it myself."

A shiver ran down the spines of those gathered, but no one dared challenge her. They knew better than to cross her.

As the group filed out, Charli stayed and asked Lolita for a minute of her time.

"I understand what you said. I just think we should consider their mental health," Lilly said, shifting nervously in her chair. "After Alex, maybe if we eased up on the restrictions—"

"Are you questioning our methods?" Lolita's voice dropped to a dangerous whisper.

"No, I just . . . some of these girls are so young. The isolation, the control . . . it's not right."

Lolita smiled, a predator sizing up prey. "You've been an excellent *house mother*, Charli. Such a shame about your sudden . . . personal emergency."

Three days later, Charli's room was empty, her personal effects gone. If anyone asked, she'd left to care for a sick relative. The message was obvious: questions weren't tolerated.

***

Lolita stared out the large office windows that overlooked her empire. The ocean, with its endless waves and shimmering surface, called to her, unaware of the darkness that pulsed in the heart of the magnificent creature she admired.

She pulled up the old video of her final gymnastics routine and watched her younger self soar through the air, precision and power in every move, until that fatal landing. Her hand drifted to her knee.

A notification pinged—another resident trying to access unauthorized websites. With practiced efficiency, she locked down their internet privileges. But for a moment, she caught her reflection in the darkened screen: the same determined set of her jaw, the same drive for perfection that had once defined her gymnastics career.

Control is safety.

Her mother's words echoing in her head. But in the quiet of her office, another thought slipped through:

At what cost?

In that moment, Lolita's transformation into the ruthless ringmaster of her own twisted circus was complete. And with every step she took away from the conference room, it became increasingly clear that there was no turning back.

***

Later that night, Lolita found herself in Tony's private quarters. The CEO reclined on a plush leather sofa, a glass of amber liquid in one hand. He looked up as she stepped into the room.

"It's bad, isn't it?" he asked, as if reading her mind.

Lolita swallowed, her usual bravado slipping for a moment. "We're in trouble, boss. I can't deny it anymore. Our movies are good, but the industry's changing, and we're being left behind."

Tony sighed, his eyes cloudy with regret. "It always comes down to this, doesn't it? One minute, we're on top of the world, and the next, we're fighting for our lives."

"We've been here before," Lolita reminded him, trying to boost her own spirits as much as his. "We'll adapt; we always do."

Tony didn't reply, and Lolita sensed his doubt. For the first time in a long time, she wasn't so sure either.

In the end, it all came down to control. They'd built their empire on the backs of others, and now, in a delicious twist of fate, they were about to be brought to their knees by the same system they'd helped create.

"What do we do?" Lolita asked, hating the desperation she heard in her voice.

Tony drained his glass before slamming it down on the table. "We do what we've always done, Lolita. We fight."

And as they sat together, two souls adrift in a sea of their own making, Lolita knew that the battle for Cum As You Are had only just begun.

As they sat there, steeling themselves for the uncertain future, rain fell outside the windows, mirroring the turmoil in their hearts. Lolita could feel the weight of their past mistakes, of all the lives they'd trampled on, bearing down on her. She knew that the path ahead would be fraught with peril, but they had no other choice. They had to try.

"We'll start by diversifying," Tony said, as if reading her mind and confirming her unspoken thoughts. "No more single source of income, no more letting others innovate, leaving us behind. You have a firm grasp of our security. Of our talent. Of our staff. We'll strengthen it further. Our talent will have no need to leave our compound, our team will see to all their needs here. We've not crossed any lines to keep up with modern tastes; we'll blur the lines if not overtly trample the ground so lines no longer exist."

Lolita nodded, her eyes on the stormy sky. "It won't be easy."

"I never said it would be," he said, a steely determination in his voice. "But we've survived worse. We can survive this, too."

They gazed at the bleak horizon together, once believing in their invincibility but now wiser. The world had changed, and they would have to change with it or perish.

And so, as the first rays of dawn crept over the horizon, signaling a new day and a new beginning, they began to plot their comeback. The phoenix would rise from the ashes.

***

"We need fresh talent," Tony mused one evening, reviewing their quarterly numbers. "Someone with star power who can help us break into new markets. And we need new content. Something that will attract the viewers who always seem to want more—"

"More what?"

"More of everything. Smaller, younger, older . . . you name it. Being extreme is the future."

Lolita's lips curved into a predatory smile. "I may have someone in mind for the new talent. Remember Justine? Word is she's fallen on hard times since leaving us."

"The redhead? Wasn't she one of your early projects? A top earner?"

"Indeed. She was more than that. She was the first one to truly challenge my system. To slip through the cracks. And now she's desperate, doing low-budget shoots just to make ends meet." Lolita's eyes gleamed with satisfaction. "The industry can be so cruel to those who try to make it on their own."

"You want to bring her back into the fold?"

"With an ironclad contract this time. No loopholes, no escape clauses." Lolita's voice hardened. "And with our new housing system, enhanced security protocols, and expanded production facilities, we can ensure she stays exactly where we want her."

Tony nodded approvingly. "This is why I made you COO. You don't just see opportunities—you create them."

"As to the *extreme* angle . . . I have a connection—"

"Legal or not," asked Tony.

"Well . . . let's just say it's a former client who manages money for a group out of Chicago. They have a stable of castoffs who might work well developing this."

Tony paused, knowing what this meant. "Do it. We've got this one chance to reinvent ourselves and return to the top. Do it."

As she left Tony's office, Lolita felt a surge of anticipation. The adult entertainment industry had given her something gymnastics never could—absolute power over others' destinies. Here, she wasn't just performing routines; she was orchestrating lives, bending wills, building an empire where her word was law.

And soon, Justine would learn firsthand just how much things had changed at Cum As You Are.

***

Lolita sat in her dimly lit office, the glow of multiple surveillance monitors casting an eerie sheen across her sculpted features. Her eyes darted from screen to screen with increasing desperation—the performers in the common area whispering in corners, security guards exchanging glances, *house mothers* huddled in conversation. When had every interaction started to look like a conspiracy?

A notification flashed on her computer: another email from that reporter asking questions about Alex. *Delete*. Another alert: unusual network activity detected. *Override*. A text from Tony about declining profits. *Ignore*.

She pulled up the latest intel on Justine—struggling with low-budget shoots, barely making ends meet. A smile curved Lolita's lips. How fitting that their prodigal daughter might soon return, this time with no chance of escape.

Rising from her chair, Lolita strode to the window that overlooked the blue Pacific waters. As the sun dipped below the horizon, fiery hues of orange and pink splashed across the sky, a breathtaking yet unsettling scene mirroring the conflict raging inside her. She stared out at the sprawling grounds, her empire of control.

Everything is perfect.

But even as the words left her lips, doubt flickered in her eyes. She had always prided herself on her ability to control every aspect of her life, but something told her the real challenges were only beginning.

Afterword

Dear Reader,

Thank you for joining Lolita on her dark and compelling journey in this origin story from the Righteous Wrong series. I hope you found her transformation from ambitious gymnast to ruthless COO as captivating and thought-provoking as I did while writing it.

As Lolita grappled with her own demons and built her empire of control, we discovered the complexity behind her seemingly villainous exterior. Her journey was not a simple fall from grace, but rather a calculated series of choices that led her down an increasingly dark path. The end result is a character whose actions we may condemn, but whose motivations we can't help but understand.

But this is only one piece of a larger narrative. In *The Emancipation Job* and other upcoming books in the *Righteous Wrong* series, we'll see how Lolita's choices impact others and ultimately lead to her confrontation with Justine and the crew who would challenge her empire. Her influence reaches far beyond these pages, setting the stage for the dramatic events to come.

So, watch for the next installments in the series and prepare yourself for more complex character studies, moral ambiguity, and the consequences of unchecked ambition. Lolita's story may begin here, but its ripple effects will be felt throughout the *Righteous Wrong* saga.

If you enjoyed this glimpse into Lolita's past, please share your thoughts on your favorite book review site. Your feedback helps shape the future of the series.

Thank you for joining me on this journey!

Walden

Acknowledgements

I am incredibly grateful for the constant and unwavering support of my family throughout my life's many adventures. Whether I was training for marathons, embarking on cross-country moves, or pouring my heart into my writing, my family has always been there, cheering me on and providing a foundation of love and encouragement.

To my wife, my partner in every sense of the word: your love, patience, and belief in me have been instrumental in all my achievements. I am so grateful to have you by my side.

To my wonderful children: your love, laughter, and endless enthusiasm have been a constant source of inspiration and joy. Watching you grow and pursue your own passions has been one of the greatest privileges of my life.

To my mother: your love, guidance, and unwavering support have shaped me into the person I am today. Thank you for always being there, through the good times and the challenging ones.

I want to express my heartfelt love and appreciation for each and every one of you. Your presence in my life has been an immeasurable gift, and I know that none of my accomplishments would have been possible without your support. You are my foundation, my inspiration, and my greatest blessing.

From the bottom of my heart, thank you.

About the author

Walden Gray has spent years exploring the intersection of justice and redemption, both in literature and in life. Like the transcendentalist thinkers who inspire their work, Gray believes in the power of individual action to effect meaningful change in the world, particularly in confronting those who exploit society's most vulnerable.

When not crafting tales of righteous wrongs and moral complexity, Gray can be found running and wandering the shores of New England's beaches, seeking inspiration in the same region that moved Thoreau and Emerson. Their writing reflects a deep appreciation for both the darkness and light in human nature, and a belief that even the most damaged souls can find their way to redemption—while shining a light on industries and organizations that profit from human suffering.

The *Righteous Wrong* series represents Gray's first venture into fiction, though they have written extensively about other topics. Through these stories, Gray aims to expose those who corrupt legitimate enterprises for personal gain, believing that fiction can be a powerful tool in revealing uncomfortable truths. They divide their time between the North Shore of Boston and various urban centers, finding that the balance between solitude and society fuels their creative process.

Gray maintains a deliberate air of privacy, believing, as Thoreau did, that *the mass of men lead lives of quiet desperation*. Through their writing, they hope to show that there are always alternatives to desperation—even if those alternatives sometimes lie outside society's traditional moral boundaries.

www.ingramcontent.com/pod-product-compliance
Lightning Source LLC
Chambersburg PA
CBHW070353130626

46556CB00007B/3154